Melted

JENNIE MARTS

DEDICATION

This book is dedicated to Todd
The one who keeps me warm on every wintry night

ACKNOWLEDGMENTS

My thanks always goes first to my husband, Todd, the one who puts up with constant chatter about plot lines and imaginary characters and the world they live in. Thank you for cooking meals, buying groceries, and putting up with me being in my pajamas, glazed look in my eyes, typing on my laptop from the time you leave in the morning until you walk back in the door from work that afternoon.

My thanks also goes out to Michelle Major and Lana Williams for your critique help, your honest feedback, and your steadfast friendship.

Thanks so much to Kristin Miller. Your friendship and plotting help is invaluable!

Special thanks goes out to Terry Gregson—my proofreader extraordinaire! So thankful for your enthusiasm and willingness to help. Thanks to Lee Cumba for always being willing to proofread.

Thank you Arran McNicol of Editing 720 for always being fast, efficient, and accommodating.

My biggest thanks goes out to my readers! Thanks for loving my stories and my characters and for asking for more. And I can't wait to share my next story with you.

1

Emily fumbled with the keys, losing her grip and dropping them in the snow. Great. Add another checkmark to her crappy day list. She tugged off her mitten with her teeth, retrieved the fallen keys, and unlocked the door of the cabin.

Her grandparents' cabin was nestled in the Rocky Mountains of Colorado, a thirty-minute drive from her apartment in Denver. It was among a half-dozen that circled a lake and that were used mainly in the summer.

The roads had been clear, but a light snow had started to fall on her way up the pass, and Emily's compact car had practically slid into the driveway of the cabin. Thick flurries now fell from the sky, covering the cabin and the surrounding trees in a blanket of sparkling white snow and ice. It was breathtakingly beautiful and only made Emily's task that much harder.

The air was still. The only sound was the light whisper of the door opening across the floor, and a flurry of snowflakes accompanied her as she stepped into the cabin. Her breath misted in the air as she turned up the thermostat, hoping the old furnace would work quickly to heat the space. The cabin consisted of a large room combining the kitchen and living area, two small bedrooms, a bathroom, and an attic loft.

Dropping her pillow and tote bag on the table, she looked around the sparsely furnished room and tried not to cry. Tonight would be the last night she'd spend in her grandparents' cabin, a place that felt as familiar to her as her own home and held the happy memories of her growing up years.

As their only child, the property had gone to her mother last spring when Nana had passed away and her mom had tried to keep up with the taxes and monthly upkeep, but just couldn't do it anymore. Not wanting to lose the cabin, Emily had scraped up enough to help with some of the bills—she'd even gone to the bank to try for a loan to buy the property itself, but couldn't make it happen.

Her mom had never been one to attach emotional significance to things, or people for that matter, if her recent divorce were any indication. She'd told Emily the property could either be a drain on all their finances or a windfall of cash, and she'd prefer the money, so she'd put the cabin up for sale. Then she'd left Emily to take care of packing it up and cleaning it out.

Her mom had been working with the realtor and taking care of the paperwork, and the new owner took over later this week. The cabin had been bought by a company called Sunshine Investments, who, according to the realtor, planned to tear down most of it and start over. Gut the place, he'd said. Modernize it.

Ridiculous. The best part of the cabin was the history, the quaint charm of the antique fixtures and the feeling you got of stepping back in time when you walked through the door.

Back into a simpler time. Before new bosses and eviction notices. Before bad breakups, and before her dad had walked out on her mom.

Crossing to the big picture window, she shed her boots and jacket as the room warmed up. Looking out across the frozen lake, she swallowed back the lump in her throat, and let the memories wash over her. Memories of summers spent here with her grandparents, swimming in the lake, making cookies, falling in love. Memories of Logan.

She'd fallen for Logan Chase the first instant she saw him.

She'd been sixteen that summer, and her parents had sent her to spend the season with her grandparents at the cabin. Her mom and dad were already having trouble back then. They were always arguing about something, and she'd been glad to escape their drama and spend the summer at the cabin.

She remembered the feeling of freedom as she'd hugged her grandparents and taken her things to the second bedroom. Not even taking the time to unpack her suitcase, she'd thrown on her swimsuit, grabbed a book, and headed for the lake. She'd heard the laughter first, a few kids messing around on the dock.

Then she saw him.

Logan had stood at the end of the dock, casually leaning against the railing. He wore a pair of cut-off jean shorts, and his skin already glowed with a healthy tan. He was tall and his dark hair was a little too long. He looked about her age and was so ridiculously cute that it almost hurt to look at him.

He saw her walking down the dock and smiled.

And that was it. She was lost. She might as well have handed him her heart, because from that one moment when he'd smiled that goofy grin at her, it belonged to him.

"Hi, guys," she'd said, fiddling with her long, dark braid and trying to sound casual as she waved at Kyle and Brooke, kids her age she knew from past summers. From the looks of the intimate playfulness between them, it seemed her friends had become a couple since she'd seen them last.

"Hi, Emily," Brooke said, giving her a hug. "We heard you were coming back for the summer." She pointed at the other two boys. "This is Logan. He just moved here. And you remember Kyle. He's my boyfriend now."

Kyle waved, more interested in checking out her bikini than making chitchat.

She'd filled out since the summer before, and she tried not to hunch her shoulders.

Logan nodded. His eyes stayed on hers as he gave her another heartbreakingly handsome smile. "Hey. Kyle might be somebody's boyfriend, but I'm not. You know, just in case you were wondering."

She'd smiled back, too tongue-tied to think of anything clever to say. She was terrible at flirting, but this boy seemed to be a pro. Great. He was probably one of those bad boys who had an old motorcycle and smoked.

But she didn't care. She just wanted to look at him, be in his presence, and have him smile at her again.

They'd spent the afternoon swimming and laughing, and by the end of that night, he'd held her hand. By the end of that week, he'd kissed her, and by the end of that summer, he'd been her first. She was head over heels in love, and the best part was that he loved her too.

Or so he'd said.

Logan was easygoing and a hard worker. He got along well with her grandparents and had a job working at the local diner with his mom. The minute he got off work, he headed for the lake to see her, and they spent most of the summer sneaking up into the loft of the cabin, talking and kissing and making plans for the future.

They used to lie on the floor of the loft and look through the slats of the banister, and watch the activity on the lake through the corner of the window. Emily loved to dream of filling the cabin wall with windows and making the loft into a bedroom where she could wake up every day to the gorgeous view.

Logan just loved to dream, period. His mom was a single parent, and she worked long shifts at the local diner. He'd always had a job, using his income to help support them. They moved around a lot, he'd told Emily, always following some great new job his mom had heard about. It was usually the same job, just in a different town, in a different restaurant.

Logan had said he dreamed of marrying Emily, and having a steady place to live and a good job. The whole white-picket-fence deal. He said he could picture it in his head, and he talked of elaborate plans of exactly what their home would look like and how many kids they would have and what kind of dog they would get.

He'd filled her head with images of a life together and promised he would love her forever. Promised they wouldn't drift apart, even though they lived in different towns. And promised that he would find her after graduation.

Except none of his promises came true. That first year, his letters and phone calls dwindled, and by the time she made it back to the cabin the next summer, he'd moved away. His mom had gotten another job and no one was exactly sure where they'd gone.

She'd spent that summer heartbroken and moody, escaping into books and spending more time with her grandmother.

Another year slipped by with no word, and by the time she left for college the next summer, she'd chalked it up as a teenage fling. She'd rationalized that it was just puppy love and they'd been kids and drifted apart, and she'd put any thoughts of Logan out of her mind. Yeah, right.

Well, she'd tried to forget him, tried to forget their time at the cabin and the promises he'd made.

Over the years, she'd moved on, studied, dated other boys, and created a life. Right now, it wasn't much of a life to brag about, but she was still here. Still getting out of bed every morning and putting one foot in front of the other.

This probably wasn't the best time to take stock of her life. She was pushing thirty, hated her job, and had just been evicted from her apartment. And now she was mooning over lost love, a teenage dream that had failed to happen. A boy that had broken her heart.

It was hard to believe that over a decade had passed since she'd seen Logan, and yet the memories were so fresh in her mind. She wondered what he would look like now. Would she even recognize him?

She shook her head. It was time to put past fantasies behind her and deal with the realities of the present. Starting now.

A shiver rolled through her as she looked out the window. The snow was falling harder, fat, fluffy flakes of white swirling in the sky. The woodbin was full, and she hoped a fire would help warm the room and chase away some of the memories.

She crumpled newspaper and stuffed it between the logs, then set small pieces of kindling on top and lit them with a match. Grandpa Hank had shown her how to build a fire. He'd shown her so many things: how to fish, how to tell which plants were poison ivy, and how to make pancakes. He'd been one of the good guys.

Grandpa had been the kind of man that gave you faith in marriage and made you believe that good men were out there. He and her grandmother had given her an example of what marriage was supposed to be like, how loyalty and love and respect were supposed to look.

Not like her parents. They were always fighting over something. She tried to stay out of it, keeping her distance and refusing to play the pawn in their latest argument. Even though they lived in the same town, she only saw her mom once every few months, and her dad less than that.

A few months back her mother had invited her for supper. Before they ate, she'd shown Emily her newly remodeled bedroom. The walls were painted pink, and silk flower arrangements and candles vomited up from every surface.

Emily had gaped at the room. "What's Dad going to think of this?"

"Who cares?" her mother had said. "He left me two months ago. We just signed the divorce papers last week."

Yeah. That was how her mother had broken the news of their divorce to her daughter, with pink walls and floral print throw pillows. How dysfunctional was that?

No wonder she didn't have a boyfriend. Between her parents' terrible example and the trust issues Logan's betrayal had given her, most of her relationships were doomed from the start.

Hopefully, the good marriage gene skipped a generation and Emily would someday find a man like Grandpa and have a shot at a marriage like he and Nana.

Which brought her back to one of the reasons she was here. She crossed the room, wiping the dust from her jeans. Digging in her tote bag, she pulled out a hammer, a flashlight, and a small crowbar, and headed to her grandparents' old bedroom.

Emily had spent a lot of time with her grandmother in her final days, and Nana had told her that she'd lost her wedding ring. The last time she'd remembered seeing it was on her nightstand in the bedroom of the cabin.

Earlier that summer, Emily had made a couple of trips up and searched the whole cabin for the ring. She'd looked under every surface and pulled out every drawer. She'd found two buttons, four dollars in change, and an issue of *Reader's Digest* from February of 1972. She'd thought she found it once, but it turned out to be a single gold hoop earring.

Frustrated, she'd almost exhausted her ideas. But the last time she'd been up here, she had moved

Nana's bed to sweep, and noticed a good-sized crack in the floorboards by the headboard. Hoping the ring had fallen through the crack, she'd brought up tools this time to check.

Somehow her quest to locate the ring had taken on a deeper meaning, as if finding it would somehow bring her closer to her grandmother or offer her the strength to let go of the cabin.

Kneeling on the floor, she wedged the claw of the hammer into the opening and pulled back. The board came loose with a loud crack, and she fell back, landing hard on her bum. *Oh crap!*

It was a good thing the inspection had already been done. *Sorry, Mr. Corporate Buyer, didn't mean to rip up part of your floor.*

What was she worried about? If Mr. Sunshine Investments was planning on gutting the place, he was probably going to rip out this floor anyway. The cheery corporate name mocked the buyer's intentions, and anger filled her as she imagined a backhoe knocking down the cabin walls.

She took a deep breath, trying to put thoughts of the evil buyer out of her head and focus on her task.

Leaning forward, she shined the flashlight into the opening on the floor. All she saw was dirt and cobwebs. There was no way she was sticking her hand down there. She took the end of the hammer and pulled it through the dirt, shining the light at the soil.

There! A glint of gold. She scratched at the dirt and unearthed a gold band. Cringing and praying a spider (or worse) didn't run over her hand, she reached down and plucked the band from the soil.

She'd found it. She couldn't believe it. Rubbing the dust from the band, she held it up, reading the inscription of her grandparents' wedding date. The ring was obviously well worn, but the gold still shone bright.

Holding back tears, she slipped the ring on her finger and held her left hand up, envisioning Nana as a young woman on her wedding date getting ready to marry the love of her life. Thoughts of Logan hovered at the edge of her mind, but she pushed them away, her focus instead on imagining what it might have been like for Nana to have been married all those years.

A lone tear escaped, running down her cheek, and her heart ached as she desperately missed her grandparents.

Thump! Thump! Thump!

The sound of loud banging on the front door of the cabin startled her.

Who the heck could that be?

She hadn't heard a car drive up, and most of the cabins were closed for the winter. Looking around for a weapon, she grabbed the hammer and stepped into the living room.

Forgetting about the ring and her grandparents, she crept to the front door, holding the hammer shakily in front of her.

Thump! Thump!

This time she jumped and let out a tiny squeal of fright. She inched to the window and peered out.

A tall man dressed in ski gear stood at the door. He wore a black cap pulled low over his forehead and a ski mask across his face. Sunglasses covered his eyes.

He held ski poles, and a set of cross-country skis lay haphazardly in the snow where it looked like he'd kicked them off.

The man pulled down his mask, exposing a scruff of dark beard. "Hello! Listen, I'm not lookin' for trouble, I just lost my dog and wondered if you'd seen it."

Oh right! The old "can you help me find my puppy?" routine. Did he have a van too? What about some candy? How dumb did he think she was?

And yet. Something about his voice seemed familiar. The way he said "trouble."

"Can you keep an eye out for him?" the man yelled. "I was cross-country skiing and he took off after a deer. He's a good dog. He won't hurt you."

It couldn't be! Not after all these years. She'd been thinking about him, surrounding herself with old memories. Her mind was just playing tricks on her.

Don't even consider opening that door.

"Okay, then. Thanks anyway." He turned, heading for his skis. Something about the way he moved. Could it be?

Her heart pounded in her chest as she yanked open the door. "Logan?"

2

A bolt of surprise hit him like a fist to the chest when Emily Wells opened the door.

He knew there'd be a chance he could run into her, but hadn't really prepared for the shock of actually seeing her. He'd thought he had every detail of her face memorized, but he hadn't seen her in so long and she'd only grown more beautiful. What was she doing here?

Of course, she would have heard about the sale of the cabin. She must have come up to clear the place out.

"Logan, is that really you?" Her voice carried volumes of pain and confusion in just a few short words.

He nodded, then cleared his throat. "Hey, Emily."

Her expression changed from confused to pissed, and that was a look he was a little more familiar with. She raised the hammer she held. *Wait, why is she holding a hammer?* "I haven't seen you in over ten years and all you've got is 'Hey, Emily'? Like you just ran to the store and got some milk?"

He shrugged. Probably not the best reaction, but he was so stunned at seeing her. He'd thought about this moment for years. Prayed he'd run into her again one day. But this particular scenario had never been in one of his fantasies. He'd never imagined the sweaty palms and the loud pounding of his heart against his chest. Or the total brain malfunction. "It's good to see you."

She shook her head in disbelief. "What are you doing here?"

"I was cross-country skiing with my dog and he ran off after a deer. I saw the lights in the cabin and thought I would check to see if he'd been through here." He shivered.

"Geez, you must be freezing." Emily frowned then took a step back. "You'd better come inside."

"I would love to, but I really need to find my dog." He looked toward the tree line and at the thickening flurries of snow. "I want to find him before the storm gets worse."

She shrugged. "Suit yourself. I'm happy to let you freeze, but Nana would be horrified with my manners if I didn't at least invite you in. And I hate to think about any dog being lost out in this storm, so if you wait a minute, I'll get my boots on and grab my jacket to help you look. So you might as well be where it's warm while you wait."

She'd always been the smarter of the two. And he *was* freezing. He hadn't meant to spend so much time skiing, then the lost dog had delayed him even more. He stepped into the warmth of the cabin. "Okay, but just for a minute." He rubbed his hands together as he looked around the living room. "This old place sure brings back a lot of memories."

A strange look crossed her face, and he couldn't read her expression. Funny, he used to always know what she was thinking.

She turned away, bending to tug her boot on, and his mouth went dry. Her figure had filled out since she was a teenager. She was a woman now, with all the right roundness in her shapely curves.

She turned around, and her eyes narrowed as if she'd just caught him in the act of checking her out. Well, she kinda had.

Before she could say anything, a huge thud hit the cabin wall and the front window filled with black fur.

"Bear!" He reached for the door.

"Bear?" She grabbed the hammer again. "Don't go out there."

Ignoring her warning, he opened the door and a huge black creature bounded into the cabin, bringing with it a blast of cold air and swirls of snow. The beast ran at Logan, planting his front paws on his shoulders and knocking him to the ground.

"Get away!" Emily screamed, brandishing the hammer.

Logan laughed, pushing the animal off of him. "Emily, it's okay. It's not *a* bear. This is my dog. His name is Bear." He gave the dog a stern look. "Bear, sit."

The giant animal sat back on its haunches. Hunks of snow-crusted black fur drooped over its eyes, and his large pink tongue hung from its mouth in a contented pant.

Logan's laughter died at the frightened look on Emily's face. "Geez, that really scared you. I'm sorry." He stood and gently took the hammer from her. He couldn't help but notice the gold wedding band on her finger, and he chided himself once again for being too late. "Bear's a Newfoundland. Sometimes I forget that other people aren't used to how big he is. He's really gentle, though. He'd never hurt you."

Her hands were shaking. Was that because of the shock of seeing him or the fright she got from the dog?

He led her to the sofa, where she eased down into the corner. Pulling the blanket from the back of the couch, he spread it out across her lap.

He sat on the edge of the coffee table across from her, and Bear padded over and plopped down on his feet.

Emily looked across at him in astonishment and blinked. "Nope, you're still here. I keep wondering if maybe I hit my head and this is just a dream." She reached out and laid her hand on his arm.

He caught his breath, surprised at the instant reaction his body still had to her slightest touch. The temperature in the room hadn't changed, yet he suddenly felt warmer. Tentatively, he laid his hand on top of hers. "I assure you that I am very real."

He shook his head. "I'm just as stunned at seeing you. You look beautiful, Em."

She pulled her hand away. "What happened to you? Where did you go? I came back the next summer and you were just gone. No one even knew where you went."

Memories of his mom and the gazillion times she'd made them move washed over him. As always, his feelings battled between a sense of betrayal that his mom should have taken better care of him and a fierce protectiveness of her. He'd heard a thousand excuses. *This is the last time. I really mean it. I know this job is gonna work out. I promise I won't drink again. I just need a little more time. Or a little more money. I love you. It's you and me against the world.*

And it had been. Until it wasn't.

He shook his head, clearing the reflections of the past. "Alaska."

"Alaska?"

He sighed. "Yep. Some guy convinced Mom that she could make really good money waiting tables up there. *Easy* money. And you know how Mom couldn't resist the allure of easy money."

"And was it? Easy money?" Emily asked the question with sincerity, not judgment. She'd always been good about trying to understand his mom instead of judging her often rotten choices.

"Was it ever?" He gave a dry laugh. "It was pretty much just terrible all the way around. It was cold and dark and I can't think of a time when I have ever been more lonely. We didn't know anyone. My mom worked all the time. We lived in this dump of an apartment with no phone, and we shared a bathroom with the couple across the hall.

"Luckily my mom hated it too. I convinced her to move to Arizona, where it was warm and sunny. Unfortunately, by that time her drinking had gotten pretty bad. I finished school in Phoenix and earned a scholarship to Arizona State. Mom took my leaving pretty hard. She fell in with a group of bikers, and I'm pretty sure her drinking progressed to drug use."

"Oh no."

"When I was in college, it was the first time I was on my own and responsible for only me. But I couldn't let go of the responsibility of taking care of my mom. I still worked and sent her money whenever I could. Even after I graduated and started my career, I would send her money to come visit or to stay with me, and she always had an excuse as to why she couldn't come. But she always took the money."

"How is she doing now?"

"She was killed in a motorcycle accident last year."

Emily's hands covered her mouth. "Oh my gosh. Logan, I'm so sorry."

He never talked about his mom. This was the most he'd said about her in years. Something about Emily got him to talking about his deepest stuff.

Bear sensed his grief and laid his massive head on Logan's lap. He shook his head and cleared his throat. "I don't know why I just told you all that stuff. I never really even talk about her. And you were the only one I ever told about her drinking. I've always felt like it was so easy to talk to you."

Emily's face looked so sad. All he wanted to do was make her smile again.

"All right, that's enough about me and my problems." He nudged her knee as he teased. "Tell me about you and how fantastic your life has been going."

She shrugged. "I certainly wouldn't call anything about my life fantastic. I just got a new boss, and he apparently liked my office better than his, because he took mine and moved me into a cubicle. My landlord decided to sell the apartment I've been renting and gave me two weeks to move out. My parents just got a divorce and my grandmother died." She gave him a cynical smile. "And oh yeah, I didn't have enough money to buy the only place in my life that felt like home, so we have to sell this cabin."

"That sucks." That was all he could think of to say. He'd listened for updates on kids or something to do with her husband, but she hadn't mentioned either. A tiny glimmer of hope sparked in his chest. "I'm sorry about Nana. I mean, I'm sorry about all that other stuff too, but I know how close you were to your grandma."

Her eyes filled with tears. "Yeah, I was. I feel like this whole chunk of my life is missing. She died last spring and I've just been kind of lost without her. I tried to scrape up enough money to buy this place myself, but we just couldn't afford to keep it." The look of sadness on her face changed to one of pure anger. "I guess some ass-hat company from out of state bought it, and the realtor told me they plan to 'gut the place.' What kind of idiot would do that?"

Wow, that was one pissed-off chick. Maybe this wasn't the best time to tell her he knew exactly who that ass-hat company was.

Before he could come up with an answer, a loud thud hit the ground outside of the cabin and Bear growled.

"What's going on, boy?" Logan got up and looked out the front window. "Oh, crap!" He waved Emily over. "You'd better come take a look at this."

3

"Was I not just telling you how great things in my life were going?" Emily asked. "Now what are we going to do about that?"

She pointed out the window to where her car now sat buried under a huge pile of snow. The weight of the snow on the roof must have gotten too heavy and slid off.

Right on to Emily's car. If it weren't for the red corner of the back end sticking out, you wouldn't be able to see the car at all.

"You got a shovel?" Logan asked.

Logan. She still couldn't believe he was here. She hadn't seen him in years, and now here he stood. In the cabin. Asking her for a shovel. As if the last several years hadn't even happened. As if he hadn't broken his promise to her. As if he hadn't left her behind. Well, she had some ideas of a few things he could do with a shovel.

Like the clumps of snow, the weight of all of her troubles suddenly felt too heavy for her shoulders to bear, and a weariness settled over her. She sighed and slumped down on the chair. "Just leave it. I'd planned to spend the night here anyway. I'll worry about it in the morning."

Logan looked at his watch then out the window at the deep snow that had accumulated. "I don't know how to say this, but it looks like you might have company tonight. I left my truck up on the ridge, and there's no way I'm going to be able to hike back up to it before it gets dark. How many sleeping bags did you bring?"

One. And the thought of sharing it with Logan both terrified and excited her. She imagined her body snuggled up against his inside the cozy sack, and her heart pounded against her chest.

Okay, mostly excited her. "I only brought one. And it's still in the car."

He laughed.

"Why are you laughing?"

Logan always did have a way of making everything into an adventure. Normally, this would be kind of funny. But she was still too freaked out that Logan was here, that her car was buried under a mountain of snow, and that this was the last night she had to spend in the cabin. To be close to Nana. Saying goodbye to the cabin would be like saying goodbye to her grandmother all over again.

"This whole thing. You. Me. Here at the cabin. It's crazy. And it kind of freaks me out." He shrugged. "You know me, I laugh at awkward situations."

"Actually, I don't know you at all anymore."

Ouch. She looked away, unable to look at the pain in his eyes. Pain that she just put there.

Why was she being so mean? That wasn't like her. She couldn't help it. She was totally out of control here, her grasp on her life was slowly slipping away, and she didn't know how to get it back.

But it wasn't Logan's fault. Well, not all of it. "Sorry, that was mean."

He shrugged again. "It's okay. And it's true. But it looks like we're going to have all night to remedy that."

All night. Here. Alone with Logan.

"It's going to get dark soon. Is there anything else in the car that you might need for tonight?"

Her stomach growled, almost as if her body were reminding her. She groaned. "The groceries. I brought up food for tonight."

"What'd you bring?"

"Hot dogs and chips. Some stuff for breakfast."

"What kind of chips?"

"Cheetos. What else?"

He grinned at her. They'd eaten bags and bags of Cheetos that summer, teasing each other about who loved them more and what exactly was in that orange powder that made them so good.

His grin widened. "I'd dig a car out of the snow for Cheetos."

A bubble of laughter burst from her before she could stop it. "Fine. Let's go find a shovel."

It took them half an hour to slog through the snow and unbury enough of the car to open the door. Emily released the front seat and pushed it forward, leaning in to get to the groceries.

"Careful. Don't fall." The feel of Logan's hands as they settled on her hips startled her, and she popped up, hit her head on the roof of the car, and fell back, against Logan. He sank backwards into the snow and she toppled into his lap.

"What were you doing?"

Logan's eyes were wide and innocent. "I was holding on to you so you wouldn't slip. I thought I was helping."

"Helping yourself. To a piece of my ass."

His eyes widened further, then his face broke into a naughty grin. "That would still be considered helping."

She narrowed her eyes at him, then swished a handful of snow at his head.

He laughed and dumped her into the snow. "Oh, that's how you want to play?"

She held up her hands in surrender. "No, Logan. I was just teasing." She crawled closer then suddenly turned to look into the trees. "What is that?"

As if responding to the alarm in her voice, Logan's head snapped toward the trees. Giving her just the vantage point she needed to dump a handful of snow down the back of his shirt.

"Hey!" He grabbed her around the middle in a playful tackle and rolled on top of her.

She shrieked in laughter, throwing snow and bucking against him.

He pinned her, breathing hard, and grinned down at her. Snowflakes stuck to his ridiculously long, dark eyelashes, and her breath caught as she looked up into his eyes.

He'd only grown more gorgeous with age. Looking at him caused her chest to actually hurt. She'd missed him so damn much.

The laughter in his eyes changed to something different. Something darker as he looked down at her lips. She sucked in her bottom lip and watched his blue eyes deepen further still.

He leaned down, his mouth achingly close to hers. She could feel the warmth of his breath against her cheek and the delicious weight of his body as he lowered himself onto hers.

What was she doing? She hadn't seen Logan in years. He might be a totally different person than she remembered him to be. He could have turned into a total a-hole. Or worse, he could still be the same sweet Logan that had held her hand and taught her how to shoot pool.

Would his lips feel familiar? Would he taste the same? Her heart pounded against her chest, and she knew her hands were trembling.

Only one way to find out.

She reached up and laid her hand against his cheek. He closed his eyes and turned his face toward her hand, softly laying a kiss against her palm.

Oh my.

She sucked in her breath, her lips aching in anticipation. He opened his eyes and looked into hers. Looked into her very soul.

Then he leaned down and took her mouth in his. He didn't just kiss her, he possessed her lips with a passion that sizzled all the way to her toes. His kisses were hungry, greedy, as if he were starving, and she was his last meal.

His right hand tangled in her hair while his left held her face, cupping her cheek in a tender grasp.

Her body burned, and she arched against him, pressing closer as she wrapped her arms around his back and held on. His back was strong. She could feel his muscles tense even through his coat.

They were putting out so much heat that she was surprised the snow hadn't melted in a circle around them.

Suddenly he pulled back, his breath now coming in hard gasps. "Wait. I'm so sorry. We can't do this." He pushed up and leaned back on the snow.

"Oh. Yeah." Her body was cold without his warmth. She shivered and wrapped her arms around her chest. "No, of course not."

Wait, why can't we?

She was so confused. Why had he stopped? Because he got caught up in the moment and then remembered he didn't actually want her? She didn't know what was happening, but she knew she didn't need this.

She rolled away and stomped through the snow to the cabin. Who cared about the food? She'd lost her appetite anyway. She was half tempted to lock the cabin door. Let him and his bear-sized dog sleep in the car.

But she didn't. She was mad, not cruel.

A few minutes later, Logan appeared in the doorway, his arms laden with everything from the back seat of her car. He dropped the sleeping bag and set several reusable grocery bags on the table. He gestured to the bags and attempted a joke. "I see you're doing your part to save the world."

"Yeah—I'm a real tree hugger, and a health nut, too. You can tell by the nutritious groceries inside my environmentally friendly bags." She unloaded the bags onto the counter, suddenly conscious of what she'd actually brought up for her overnight stay.

She had a package of hot dogs, some buns, a family-size bag of Cheetos, a box of sugary cereal, milk, a small chocolate cake, a can of whipped topping, and two bottles of wine.

Logan looked over her shoulder at the lineup of goods. "Just exactly what kind of party were you planning tonight and how many were invited?"

She turned on him, feeling the anger coming off her in waves. "A pity party for one." She grabbed the bottle of wine off the counter and twisted the lid off. She was so broke that she had to resort to drinking wine that came with a twist-off lid. That thought made her even angrier.

She tipped the bottle to her lips and took a slug before turning back to Logan. "And you're crashing my party."

He held his hands up in surrender. "Okay. Okay. Listen, Emily, I'm sorry. About the kiss. I'm just not that kind of guy."

She took another gulp of wine. "What kind of guy is that, Logan? One that kisses girls he supposedly used to be in love with? Or the kind of guy who leads girls on and then breaks their hearts?"

"No. What are you talking about?" He stepped up to her, taking the bottle of wine and setting it on the counter. "Emily, I'm not the kind of guy that kisses another man's wife."

She hadn't eaten lunch, and she could feel the wine taking hold. "What are you talking about? Whose wife did you kiss?"

He picked up her hand, the one still wearing her grandmother's ring. "Your husband's."

She shook her head, wishing she hadn't drunk that wine so quickly. "What do you mean? I'm not married."

A look of shock crossed his face. "But you're wearing a ring. And when I came to find you at college, your roommate told me you were engaged and getting married." He shook his head. "Wait, what do you mean by *supposedly* in love with?"

She put her hand on his chest. "Hold on. Did you say you came to find me?"

"Of course I did. I told you I would."

"You came to my college? Why didn't you talk to me?" She couldn't believe what she was hearing. He'd really come for her?

"I tried. I showed up at your room, with flowers and sweaty palms, the whole nine yards. I'd saved for months to get the bus fare up to Colorado and couldn't wait to surprise you. I was terrified you'd forgotten me or wouldn't want to see me, but I sure wasn't prepared for you to be engaged."

He was terrified she wouldn't want to see him? That was crazy. She'd waited two years for him. "I wasn't engaged. Who told you that?"

"I talked to your roommate. She told me you were super serious with this guy, that you were crazy in love and getting married. I couldn't believe it. I kept asking her if you were really happy, and she insisted that you were. I was crushed."

"But why didn't you still come find me? Ask me yourself?"

He shrugged. "I don't know. I had this whole plan in my head of how excited you would be to see me, then I was so shocked that you were engaged, I didn't know what to do. I was young and stupid and hurt. I threw the flowers in the trash and got back on the bus. Then spent the next ten hours regretting that I didn't find you myself. Talk to you. See your face, at least."

"And that was it? You never tried again? Never looked for me on social media? Checked out my profile? It would have been so easy to see that I never got married."

He gave her an "are you serious?" look. "I don't have time to mess around with all the face-tweet stuff. Besides, why would I want to see photos of you and the life I was supposed to have had with you? Knowing you were happy was enough. I didn't need to torture myself with more proof that I was an idiot to take so long to get back to you."

"I can't believe this." She sank into the kitchen chair, still stunned. "All this time, I thought you'd lied about your feelings for me. Broke your promise about coming back for me. I was with a guy in college, but thanks to you and my dad, I had terrible trust issues and we broke it off. My college roommate was a hag. She hated me and took every opportunity to make my life miserable. She never even told me you'd been there." Her voice trembled with emotion and too much wine, and she could feel the tears filling her eyes.

"Hey, hey. Don't do that." Logan bent down beside her and pulled her into his arms. He tucked her head into his shoulders and rubbed his hand along her back. "Don't cry. You know I can't handle it when you cry."

It felt so good to be held by him. To be back in Logan's arms. He'd grown taller since they were sixteen, and his muscles had filled out. Oh, how his muscles had filled out. She clung to him, the roller-coaster emotions of the day churning in her chest. A hard sob escaped her, and she cried into his shoulder.

Cried for the loss of her grandmother and the cabin she had always called home, cried for the pain of her dad walking out on her mom, and all the futile anger she had spent on him and every other man that had disappointed her in her life.

And she cried for Logan, for the years they had wasted, for the misplaced anguish she'd felt over him not keeping his promise, and for the heartache of not being able to believe their love had been real.

"Shhh. It's okay." He murmured soft words into her ear and simply held on to her. He had always been good about letting her cry it out.

She took a deep breath and wiped at her eyes. "I'm okay." She tilted her head back and smiled at him. "You know how I get."

He grinned. "Yeah. I know you get so much stuff bottled up in you that sometimes you just need to have a good bawl and get it out." He touched the corner of her lip. "And I always knew if I just shut up and held you through it, you would come out of it with a smile."

Over the past few years, she'd hardened her heart as solid as the chunks of ice forming in the snow outside of the cabin. Like the ice, she'd frozen out any attempts to love again, to trust a man to keep his word. It was easier that way. Easier to keep her feelings at bay than to risk the pain of her heart breaking again.

But Logan's hand on the side of her face, his reassuring smile, the way he knew just what she needed, were all working to melt the icy edges of her frozen heart. Warmth flowed through her, starting at the corner of her lip where his thumb rested.

She smiled up at him, felt her whole face beam with happiness.

He grinned back. A grin that she recognized with every fiber of her being. He might be taller, his hair might be darker, and he might have a beard, but he was still Logan. He leaned forward, and she burned with the anticipation of his kiss.

He stopped and gave her a sideways glance. "So, you're *really* not married?"

She laughed. "I am really not married. This is my grandmother's ring. I just found it in the bedroom and had slipped it on to feel close to her. I am totally single."

His eyes narrowed, going dark with desire. "No, you're not. Not anymore." He leaned in, this time not stopping, but moving slower. His hand still cupped her face, and he ran his thumb along her bottom lip before gently grazing it with his lips. A whisper-soft kiss. A taste of what was to come.

She shivered. A delicious shiver of expectation.

He pulled back. "Geez, Em. You're shivering. You must be freezing." He stood and pulled her up then rubbed her arms. "We need to get you into some dry clothes."

No, actually, she would be fine if she just got out of her clothes altogether.

Wait. Hold up. This *was* going way too fast. He was right. She needed to get into some dry clothes, take a minute to think. With her head, not her lust-crazed body. She knew Logan as a boy, but she knew next to nothing about him as a man.

She reached for her tote bag. "I brought some pajamas to change into." She looked down at Logan's soaked ski pants. "What about you? Don't you want to take those off and get dry?"

He gave her a sheepish grin. "Yeah, that's gonna be a little bit of a problem. I hadn't planned on being out all night. All I'm wearing under these is a t-shirt and my underwear."

Oh boy.

She scoffed, trying to sound casual. "Don't be ridiculous. It's more important for you to get dry and warm. I can handle you in underwear. We spent the entire summer together wearing nothing but our swimsuits."

He pulled at the zipper, the soft sound of the releasing metal sending a seductive thrill down her spine.

"Wait." She covered her eyes with her hand, her bravado gone and suddenly feeling like the shy teenager she used to be. "Boxers or briefs?"

He chuckled. "Uh…boxers, I guess."

She heard the sound of the slick ski pants hit the floor and peeked between her fingers.

Holy hotness!

"Those aren't boxers," she croaked. "Those are boxer briefs. There's a difference." And in Logan's case, it was a *big* difference.

She tried to swallow, but her mouth had gone totally dry at the sight of Logan standing in front of her, wearing only a t-shirt and a pair of tight black boxer briefs. His body was muscled and toned and didn't show an ounce of fat.

Her infrequent times at the gym didn't erase the midnight raids of the freezer for ice cream, and she was suddenly self-conscious of her rounded figure.

The last time Logan had seen her, she'd had the body of a sixteen-year-old girl.

She grabbed her tote and headed for the bathroom. "I'll be back," she said before closing the door.

She shrugged out of her wet clothes and wished she had worn better underwear. Especially because her plain black bikinis showed through the worn fabric of the red and white striped pajama pants she'd brought. She slipped on the short red t-shirt and looked at herself in the mirror.

Her face was flushed, framed by her long, dark hair. Okay, she had great hair, but she was suddenly hypercritical of everything else about herself. And for goodness' sake, why had she brought these old pajamas?

Everything seemed too snug, the knit fabric of her pants hugging every curve. The V-neck of her t-shirt dipped too low, displaying her deep cleavage and the edges of her black lace bra. At least she'd worn a good bra. But she didn't want to seem like she was flaunting it.

She had a hoodie in another bag that she could zip up over her pajamas, but she still had to cross the living room to get to it.

She hung her wet clothes over the shower rod to dry then cautiously stepped out of the bathroom.

Logan knelt by the fire, adding another log. The firelight only accentuated his body, showing off his muscled arms. All of her woman parts clenched in desire, and her mind filled with dirty little thoughts about how he could "light her fire."

He must have heard the door, because he turned to look at her. His eyes widened, and she thrilled at the way he had to swallow before he spoke.

She stepped closer. Maybe she wouldn't get her hoodie just yet.

He grinned. "You look like a candy cane in those pants."

Oh Lord! A candy cane? Now all she could think about was places that he could lick her.

She could think of nothing to stay. No snappy comebacks. A log shifted in the fire as she stood silently, looking at Logan and aching with want.

Before either of them could speak, a soft pop sounded, and the power went out.

4

"Thank goodness I just added another log to the fire." Logan could see Emily standing in the dim firelight, and moved toward her. "Do you think there's still some candles around here?"

"Yeah, I left some in the kitchen drawer." Emily pulled her phone from her bag and touched the screen, and a bright light shone from the top of it.

She smiled. "Flashlight app. The reception is so spotty up here that I don't know if I could make a call, but I can get the flashlight and calculator to work. And we could probably play a few games of *Candy Crush* before my battery dies."

Don't say candy. Those red and white striped pants she was wearing already reminded him of peppermint. They were killing him. He ached for the taste of her again. He didn't need to imagine her as a piece of candy too.

Why did he feel like such an awkward teenager around her again? He couldn't believe he'd said that. What kind of an idiot tells a girl she looks like a candy cane? What a dumb thing to say. But she did look good enough to eat.

His stomach growled at the thought of eating. His cross-country skiing schedule hadn't really gone as planned, and he'd missed lunch. Making them something to eat would be a good thing to focus on instead of the way that t-shirt dipped in the front and hugged her lusciously curved body. "We should probably save the battery in case we can't dig out tomorrow. Why don't you get some candles going, and I'll figure out how to roast some hot dogs."

"Sounds like a plan."

They worked together in companionable silence. Emily set up candles around the living room area and Logan focused on putting together makeshift roasting sticks. She brought the grocery sacks over and set them on the floor by the fire.

She dragged the coffee table to the side and pulled the sofa closer to the fire then made a nest of the sofa cushions and sleeping bag. Plopping down beside him, she patiently waited for Bear to settle in next to her then patted his large head as he laid it by her knee.

Pulling out the two bottles of wine, she held them up for his inspection. "Which goes better with Cheetos? Red or white?"

He laughed as he threaded hot dogs onto the sticks and held them over the flames. "Well, I have a pretty discriminatory taste when it comes to my wine." He put on a fake English accent. "I think the woodsy tones of the white will really bring out the cheesy flavor of the orange dust on the puffs."

She giggled as she twisted the lid off and handed him the opened bottle of white wine. "Your accent is terrible."

He took a swig of the wine and grimaced. "So is this wine."

"I know. What can I say? I'm broke and was depressed. I wasn't getting it for the refined flavor."

She laughed and took a sip, then set the bottle on the floor between them. He watched her lean back against the pillows. She looked relaxed and happy as she casually gathered her long hair and twisted it into some kind of knot on top of her head.

She still had amazing hair. It'd felt like silk in his hands when he'd kissed her earlier. And now, with it pulled up, tendrils of loose curls falling free of the tousled knot, it made her look young and more carefree. Less stressed and nervous around him.

And sexy as hell. "God, you're beautiful."

Her eyes widened in surprise at his compliment then softened, and he swore her cheeks tinged with a touch of pink. "I was just thinking the same thing about you."

Feelings of desire churned in his stomach. He longed to lay her down on the sleeping bag, pull her hair free, and strip her of the candy-striped pants.

A soft whoosh sounded. Emily shrieked and pointed at the fire, where his roasting stick and hot dog was engulfed in a bright red flame. "Your wiener's on fire!"

He pulled the hot dogs from the fire and blew out the flame before giving her a funny look. "Did you really just say that?"

She nodded then burst into a fit of giggles, hiding her face in her hands. He chuckled as he watched her body shake with laughter. Holding her sides, she let out a tiny snort, which set off another round of giggles. She tried to catch her breath, but was still laughing too hard.

He laughed with her, knowing the joke was juvenile, but her joy was contagious, and it felt so good to have a good laugh. The kind that made your belly hurt and your cheeks sore.

His laughter eased, and he shook his head. "Nobody cracks me up the way you do. I've missed laughing with you."

"I've missed you too."

He slid the hot dogs into buns, taking the burned one for himself. He wouldn't taste it anyway. How could he think about food when his appetite yearned for a difference kind of feast? He passed her the hot dog. "Your wiener, madame," he said with a flourish, setting her off on another round of hysterical giggles.

They talked and laughed as they ate hot dogs and fed each other Cheetos. They were silly together, as people who'd known each other since they were kids often were. Emily giggled as she fed two raw hot dogs to Bear, who wolfed them down in one bite. It felt good to see her playful and relaxed.

Logan was having one of the best nights he could remember, but he definitely wasn't relaxed. Every nerve cell in his body was taut with energy and sent zings of sensation through him every time her hand brushed his or her leg bumped up against him.

He was hyperaware of her every movement, the way she smelled, the way tendrils of her hair lay against her neck, the way he could see right down her shirt every time she bent forward.

They'd finished a bottle of wine and half of the cake, then his heart stopped as he watched her tip the can of whipped topping and squirt it into her mouth. She caught him watching and gave him a devilish grin, a tiny dollop of white cream at the corner of her mouth. He yearned to lean forward and lick the silky whipped cream from her lips.

He'd been on plenty of dates, been with his share of women, but something about Emily made him feel gawky and clumsy, like his arms and legs weren't connected right to his body. He felt nervous and excited at the same time, and wondered if she noticed how many times he'd laughed too loud or awkwardly in the wrong place.

But as self-conscious as he felt, he also felt completely and totally right. Like this was exactly where he was supposed to be, in this cabin, on this night, with this beautiful girl.

He leaned back on the sofa, pulling out the old "stretch and then casually rest your arm on her shoulders" move. She curled into him, laying her head on his shoulder, and he felt his whole body relax into hers.

He reached up, pulled her hair from the topknot, and sucked in a breath as he watched it fall, the long, dark curls cascading around her shoulders. He picked up strands of it, running the silky locks through his fingers. He released the breath slowly. He was cool. No big deal.

Wait. The hand that she so casually had rested on his chest now started making slow circles of caress on his chest. Forget smooth and relaxed, his body just shifted gears and swung into overdrive.

"So tell me about what you do now?" she asked, her voice calm and easy, as if she had no idea the kind of turmoil she was stirring up inside of him. "What did you major in at college?"

"Er...um...architecture. I've been working for a company in Arizona, but I have my own firm now."

"I can see that. You always did like to talk about building things."

What? An architect? Her hand slid under his shirt and traced a circle around his belly button. Her fingers were cool against his skin, which felt like it was on fire from her touch. This seemed like a great segue into telling her he'd been the one to buy the cabin. To share with her his plans for renovation.

"So, I've been wanting to tell you—"

Her hand moved lower, her fingers dancing along the edge of the elastic band of his briefs, and all thought left his brain.

She looked up at him, her brown eyes gorgeous in the firelight. "Yes? You wanted to tell me something?"

Uh? Did he? He'd been about to say something. But it was gone now.

All he could think about was her hands on his bare skin, sliding lower, and the way her eyes went soft and her lips parted as if in invitation.

He didn't take the time to RSVP, he just leaned down and kissed her. No gentle brush of his lips, but a siege of passion as he covered her mouth. She tasted like chocolate and wine, and she moaned against his mouth.

His self-control shattered. He had to have her. He feasted on her mouth while filling his hands with her lush curves. Squeezing, caressing, he explored her body with his hands, his lips, his tongue, drawing pleasure from each gasp of delight.

He nuzzled her neck, tangling his hands in her hair as he laid a fiery trail of kisses down her throat and into the vee between her breasts. Raising her t-shirt, he traced the lacy outline of her bra with his tongue while his hands frantically worked the clasp at her back. With a twist of his fingers, the hooks released, freeing her full breasts.

It wasn't enough. In seconds, he had her shirt pulled off and had tossed her bra across the floor. He looked down at her as she lay under him, her breasts bare and her skin glowing in the firelight. She was magnificent.

And she was his. For that moment, she belonged to him. And he planned to have her. Every inch of her.

His pulse quickened as he bent his head, teasing her swollen nipples with his tongue, his lips. She arched under him, bucking against his hips with her own need.

He loved the little sounds she made, the sighs, the gasps, the quick cries of pleasure she offered him when he discovered a new spot to taste.

His appetite for her was insatiable, yet she seemed just as hungry for him. He swore he could feel the blood pounding in his veins as she groped for his t-shirt and tugged it over his head. She wiggled out of the pajama pants and bikini panties, and his breath caught at the beauty of her naked body.

She was no longer a teenage girl with spindly arms and gangly legs. She was now a woman with lush curves and ripe, full breasts, her skin soft and supple. And she knew how to use her body to seduce and please, to lead him down a seductive path of pleasure and desire.

He paused, his pulse racing as he explored her body with his gaze. "You are stunning."

She smiled up at him, not shying away, and he loved the brazen look she gave him. "I'm not a teenager anymore."

He grinned. "I know. I like you much better as a woman." His comment earned him another grin.

"Em, I have loved you since the day I laid eyes on you walking down that dock. Thoughts of you have filled my head, my dreams, my fantasies since I was sixteen years old. I don't know what crazy twist of fate finally brought us back together, but I don't want to waste another minute of my life being without you."

A flicker of doubt crossed her face. "Logan, this is all happening so fast. We don't have to talk about the future. I'm happy being with you right now. I've dreamed about this moment for years, wondering what you would be like as a man. Would your voice be lower? Would you be taller?"

"How does the real me measure up to that fantasy guy?" He asked the question with apprehension, a touch of worry in his tone.

He needn't have worried. She ran her fingers along his bearded chin, sending an electric thrill down his spine. "The real you is better than I ever could have imagined."

A low chuckle sounded in his throat. Thank goodness for that.

He took her face in his hand, cupping her cheek in his palm. "Emily, it doesn't matter if we talk about it now or tomorrow or a month from now. I finally have you back in my life and I'm not letting you go again. I gave you my heart when we were sixteen, but now I'm prepared to offer you my body and soul. I belong to you. I always have."

He sounded like a lovesick boy. He couldn't believe the words tumbling from his mouth. But he meant them. Every syllable. He held his breath as he waited for Emily to either save his ego or destroy him altogether. With one word, she could wreck him, damage his already fragile heart, or she could restore him, mend the brokenness inside of him.

In the dim firelight, he watched her eyes fill with tears, watched her fight some kind of inner struggle, and he held his breath as he waited to see which side would win. She spoke, her voice barely above a whisper. "I'm scared."

He smiled. "Scared? *You're* scared? I'm terrified. I just told a girl that I haven't seen in years that I'm still in love with her. Babe, I just handed you my heart, and now I'm waiting to see if you'll take it or rip it from my chest and crush it to bits."

Oh my gosh. He needed to stop talking. He sounded like such a dork.

"I'll take it." She smiled, and his heart soared. He felt like beating his chest in triumph. He really was a nerd.

Instead he kissed her. He stopped talking and showed her how he felt. This time, he kissed her slowly, ran his hands over her in tender caresses, drawing out the temptation, reveling in the smoldering tension lying just below the surface.

She responded with an urgent need, a desperate passion that spoke volumes to his wounded heart.

He answered her demands, quickening the pace, their bodies melding together in a dance as old as time. They knew the rhythm, had danced this same melody, in this same place, but in another time.

This time the music was just a little different, the harmony was sweeter, and the measure of the tempo a little slower, more deliberate as they moved in rhythm to a song only their hearts could hear.

5

Emily woke to the sun streaming in the window. Her body ached from sleeping on the floor, her muscles tender and sore from the night spent in Logan's embrace. She smiled, replaying exactly what had caused the soreness, and rolled toward him. His body was warm—and furry. Ugh. Not Logan.

She sat up, still naked and instantly cold. The fire smoldered, giving off little heat. Bear rolled toward her, hoping for a scratch, but Logan was nowhere in sight.

Great. He got what he wanted and ditched her. She should have known. Typical man behavior.

Wait. This wasn't a regular one-night stand. She knew Logan. He had opened up to her last night.

Besides, he wouldn't leave his dog.

The bathroom door opened and Logan emerged, already dressed in his ski clothes. He was whistling a happy tune and when he saw her, and a huge smile lit his face. "Good morning, sunshine."

"Good morning." She pulled the sleeping bag up around her chest and ran her hands through her hair. Things that looked beautiful by firelight tended to not look the same in the harsh light of day. "I must look a mess."

He crossed the room, knelt beside her, and gave her a quick kiss. "You look amazing."

She laughed, secretly loving the compliment. "You need glasses." She gestured to his ski clothes. "Are you going somewhere?"

"Yeah. It stopped snowing sometime last night, so I thought I'd try to hike up to my truck. If I can make it, I'll drive it down here then help you uncover your car. If you can't get out, at least I've got four-wheel drive in my truck and can get us back to town."

The real world slammed into her, reminding her that this was her last day at the cabin, that she needed to finish packing up the last few things and say her final goodbyes.

Logan had already stood, and was putting on his coat. "I'll take Bear with me and hopefully make it back in a couple of hours." He crossed to the door and called the dog. "When I get back, I have something I want to show you."

She gave him a sardonic grin. "Oh, really?"

He laughed. "Not that. Well, maybe that. Yeah, probably that. But something else too." He shook his head and reached for the door. "I'm leaving before I get myself into any more trouble."

Before closing the door, he leaned back in. "And Emily, I *am* coming back for you."

She smiled and hugged herself as the door shut behind him.

Taking advantage of the time, she ate some cereal and brushed her teeth. She took a shower, combing out her hair and letting it air-dry.

It was good to have the time to herself to clean up and collect the final things that had belonged to her grandmother. As she finished packing the last box, the electricity came back on with a soft whir of sound and the restored steady hum of the refrigerator.

Her cell phone had died sometime in the night, and she dug the cord out of her bag and plugged in her phone to charge. Within a few seconds of charge, her phone beeped out the signal that she had texts waiting.

Picking up the phone, she saw two missed messages. The first was from her mom checking to see how she was doing with the final cabin farewell, and the second was from the realtor.

She opened the second text. It was a long message detailing the final instructions for the closing. She scrolled to the bottom, scanning the words. Her heart stopped as she read the name of the owner of Sunshine Investments.

Logan Chase.

It couldn't be. Why wouldn't he have told her?

She knew why. Because she was an idiot. He had used her. Taken advantage of her and their shared history to get in a night of easy sex before he claimed the cabin and tore it down. He'd said he was an architect. He probably planned to build a shopping mall or a tourist attraction here.

How could she have been so stupid? She'd let her guard down for one minute, and look what happened. He was probably laughing at her right now. Having a good old chuckle at her expense. How could she have believed that he still had feelings for her after all these years?

But she still had feelings for him.

Silencing the small voice inside her head that told her to wait for Logan, she crammed her feet into her boots and shoved her arms into her coat.

She grabbed one of the boxes and her tote, carried them to her car, and stuffed them into the back seat. Some of the snow had melted off her car, and she attacked the rest with the ice scraper, flinging snow and chunks of ice into the air.

She poured her rage into clearing the car, and her forehead was damp with sweat by the time she'd freed the car from its snowy prison.

The sound of an engine had her turning, and a large blue truck pulled into the driveway behind her car. Logan climbed out, and Bear jumped from the cabin and ran to her, wagging his tail in a joy-filled greeting.

Logan jogged through the snow, a happy grin on his face. "Hey, Em, I told you I'd be back."

His smile fell as he registered the anger on her face. "Emily, I can explain."

"Oh, can you?" she yelled. "You can explain how you have spent the last twenty-four hours with me and failed to mention the fact that *you* are the ass-hat that's taking away my grandmother's cabin? You didn't fail to get me naked, but you were certainly unsuccessful at passing along that happy bit of news."

"Emily, please."

She held up her hand and stomped back into the cabin to get the rest of her things. She heard Logan slam the door of his truck and follow her in.

Turning on him, she let loose the anger that had been building since she'd read the text. "You seriously couldn't find the time to tell me you were the buyer? How about when you first walked in and I told you why I was here? Or how about when I was crying on your shoulder?"

She shook her head, fighting the hot tears that threatened to spill out. "You must have thought I was a real idiot. You let me cry, patted my back, then thought you could get a quick lay before you kicked me out and tore the cabin down. I was such a fool to trust you again."

"Emily, stop." His voice held a hard edge to it. "Don't ever say that to me again. I would *never* use you, and if you think that's the kind of man I've become, then you never really knew me at all."

A ring of truth sounded in his words, but it was too late. He'd betrayed her again, just like she knew he would. Just like he'd done before.

Except he hadn't before. He'd kept his word. He'd come back for her. Just like he said he would.

Her shoulders fell and she slumped into the chair, exhausted and confused. She didn't know what to believe anymore.

Logan set a black bag on the table and pulled his laptop from it. "I told you I wanted to show you something. I'd like to show you the plans I have for the cabin." He opened the computer and fired it to life. After clicking a few keys, he turned the screen toward her.

She swiped at the errant tear that had escaped down her cheek, and turned to the screen. It wouldn't hurt to look.

Logan pointed to the plans, explaining what she was seeing. "Emily, I'm not tearing down the cabin. I'm just renovating it, making it a little more modern. You said that this place was the only place that ever truly felt like home to you—well, that's how I feel about it too. My mom moved us around so many times that I never knew if I was coming or going. But something about this place was special."

He looked over at her. "Maybe because it was the first place I ever really felt loved. Plus, your grandparents were good to me. Your grandpa taught me to fish, and Nana was always slipping me cookies and sandwiches to take home. I love this cabin. I would never do anything to take away the charm or the personality."

Pointing to the screen, he kept going, his words coming out in a rush, as if he were afraid she would leave if he stopped talking. "You can see here, all I'm doing is updating the wiring and adding a more updated furnace and hot-water heater. I planned to update the kitchen by bringing in some more modern appliances, but I want to keep the rustic feel."

Emily tried to make sense of what he was showing her. "But the realtor said you were going to gut the place, tear down walls."

Logan pointed to the wall that faced the lake. "I am going to tear out part of that wall. But just to replace it with windows. You once said you wished that whole wall was filled with windows so you could look out and see the lake."

He'd remembered.

He clicked the keyboard, and a new picture flashed on the screen. "And see here, I planned to build a bedroom in the loft, just like you always wanted."

Like she'd always wanted? She couldn't believe that he'd remembered her wishes for the cabin. "But why? Why would you make this the way I wanted? You said you thought I was married, so I would probably never even see what you did."

"It didn't matter. I was happy here. Looking back on my childhood, this is the only place I truly felt happy. When I decided to branch out into my own company, I realized that I could work from anywhere, and the first place that I thought of was here. I started checking around, and when I heard the cabin had come up for sale, I knew I had to buy it. Then I started thinking about how to fix it up and how to make it the way we'd always dreamed it would be."

He picked up her hand. "Emily, I always felt like I failed you. That I didn't make it back in time. That I missed my shot at having a life with you. But this was my small way of making it up to you. Even if you never knew, *I* would know that I kept the cabin from going to strangers. To someone who really could tear it down."

He shrugged. "And yeah, maybe I hoped that when you saw that I was the buyer, I would get a chance to see you again. But I love this cabin." He looked up at her, pain evident in his eyes. "And I still love you. It kills me that you would even think that I would use you. Last night was amazing. One of the best nights of my life. I was so happy that I found you again and that you still cared about me."

He still loved her. He still wanted to be with her. Even after she'd said those terrible things to him, flung those awful accusations. She shook her head. "But why didn't you just tell me?"

He sighed. "Because I'm an idiot. I wanted to. But you were so happy to see me and so mad at the guy that bought it. I didn't want that guy to be me. Then later, I was going to tell you, when we were in front of the fire, and I told you I'd become an architect."

"So, why didn't you?"

A sheepish grin covered his face. "I started to, but then you touched me *there*. And when you touch a guy *there*, they lose all cognitive ability to think or reason."

She laughed. A big, shoulder-shaking laugh. "You are an idiot." She stood up and slid her arms around his neck. "But you're *my* idiot."

He raised an eyebrow at her. "Yeah?"

"Yeah."

She looked at this man, and her heart flip-flopped in her chest. She still saw the boy that he was, but now she saw the man he'd become. The man who'd kept his promise. Who had purchased her family's cabin because it had felt like his home too. Who'd hugged her while she cried and told her he still loved her. Who had made love to her in the light of the fire and then held her as she'd slept.

She had spent so many years building a wall of defenses around herself, not letting anyone in. Now Logan was back, and like the sunshine on the snow outside, he was melting the frozen pieces of her wounded heart. Did she dare risk her fragile heart again? Could she trust Logan to guard it and protect it?

He kissed her then, a sweet, tender kiss, full of promise. Then he took her hands from around his neck and held them as he knelt on one knee, a look of love shining in his eyes.

Wait. What was he doing? Her heart stopped. A minute ago she was worried about her heart being too cold, but now it was frozen altogether.

She stared at him, afraid to even breathe.

"Listen, Em, I know this seems sudden, but I have loved you for over half of my life. I've already wasted too many years without you, and I don't want to waste another day, another minute."

He smiled at her, a gorgeous grin that shot straight to her heart. "I want to marry you. To build a life with you. I want you to quit that crappy job that you hate and move up here. Help me renovate the cabin. Help me make it into a home. Our home." He squeezed her hand, rubbed his thumb along the gold band of Nana's ring. "I want us to live a life like your grandparents had, have the kind of marriage that they showed us was possible. Emily Wells, would you do me the honor of becoming my wife?"

She couldn't breathe, couldn't speak, couldn't move. Then the warmth of his words melted the last frozen pieces of her heart and her face broke into a grin. A small laugh bubbled out of her, almost like a hiccup. She nodded, willing her lips to move. "Yes."

"Yes?" His face beamed with sheer happiness.

"Yes. I will marry you."

He whooped with joy. Standing up, he wrapped her in a hug, lifting her off her feet, then planted a kiss on her laughing lips. "You have made me the happiest man on earth."

He set her down, his face flushed and his words coming out in a rush. "Listen, I don't want to pressure you, we don't have to do it today or even tomorrow, but how about next week? Are you free on Thursday? Would you marry me next Thursday? We could do it here at the cabin."

A Thursday wedding, in the middle of winter, at her grandparents' cabin? Not exactly the dream wedding she'd always pictured. But then, nothing in her life had gone as she'd imagined.

She thought she would never find love again, never have a chance at the kind of marriage that her grandparents had shared. She'd thought she'd lost both Logan and the place she had always called home. But instead she got both. Happiness filled her as she looked into Logan's eyes then leaned up to kiss him.

Yes, Thursday sounded just fine.

THE END

Did you love this story?

If you enjoyed this book, try ***Icing On The Date***—
the first book in the Bannister Brothers Books series.
Professional hockey player Owen Bannister, meets
Gabby Davis—the sexy caterer who is about to
change his entire game. She's cooking up romance
and their passion is hot enough to melt the ice. Owen
learns that love is the ultimate game changer and he's
about to get checked.

***

Keep Reading for an excerpt to *ICING ⌣ DATE*:

ICING ON THE DATE

She scrolled through the contacts. Had he said Bane or Ben? Her eyes caught the word Bane, and she pressed the contact and held the phone to her ear.

A sleepy male voice answered. "Dammit, Owen. I told you I'm not coming out tonight."

"Um. Hello. Is this Owen's brother?"

"Who's this?" The voice went instantly alert. "Where's my brother?"

"This is Gabby Davis. I'm a caterer, and I'm working a party at the Crown Hotel downtown. I'm in the women's bathroom on the first floor, and your brother appears to be very drunk and passed out on my lap. He asked me to call you. He seems to think he's in some kind of trouble."

"Oh, he's in a whole hell of a lot of trouble. Listen, Gabby, thank you for calling me. I can be there in fifteen minutes. Can you stay with him until I get there?"

"Sure, I guess." She wasn't in charge of the whole catering job tonight—only the desserts—and no one would notice she was missing as the party wound down.

"I'm on my way. Keep him out of sight and in the bathroom if you can."

Out of sight of whom? *What kind of trouble was this guy mixed up in?*

"I can try."

"I'd really appreciate it, Gabby. You have no idea how much I appreciate it. Tell him I'm on my way." He hung up.

Gabby set the phone down. "Your brother's on his way. How about if I just sit here with you until he gets here?" The guy was big and his brother had said he was in trouble, but she wasn't afraid. He didn't seem dangerous, even with the bruised black eye.

He snuggled into her chest, smearing remnants of chocolate frosting across his cheek. "Are you an angel? 'Cause you smell like heaven," he slurred. "Seriously, why do you smell so damned good? Like cookies and cake and chocolate?"

He opened his eyes and squinted at her chest. He ran a finger along the top edge of her breast, sending a wave of tingles darting down her spine, and came away with a dab of frosting on the end of his finger tip. Popping his finger into his mouth, he groaned in pleasure. "God, you even taste like chocolate. I just want to frickin' lick you."

Wow. Wildly inappropriate to say, but the words still sent a prickle of desire through her. This crazy hot guy just told her he wanted to *lick* her. Granted, it was a drunken statement and he most likely meant the chocolate frosting spread across the front of her shirt, but it had been a long time since she'd had a man tell her anything half as remotely sexy as that statement had been.

Spending all of her time working, saving money, and taking care of her miscreant brother didn't leave a lot of time for dating, and she didn't want to think about how long it had been since anything of hers had been licked.

If you enjoyed this story, be sure to check out all of Jennie Marts' books, including the adventures of the Page Turners book club:

Another Saturday Night and I Ain't Got No Body - Book 1
Sunny Vale considers herself a dog-loving, romance-reading, homebody. But her life goes from dull to deadly when her book club fires her from her own love life and sets her up on six blind dates—one of whom might be with a murderer.

Easy Like Sunday Mourning - Book 2
When single mom Maggie Hayes decides to try dating again, a cute video game-designing nerd seems like a safe bet….until he becomes the prime suspect in a murder. Maggie must learn to trust again while playing the most dangerous game of all.

Because defeat could mean not only losing her heart, but also her life…

Just Another Maniac Monday - Book 3
Edna Allen's Monday goes from mundane to murderous when she opens the front door to find the love of her life standing there. A man she thought had died years ago… after being accused of murder. As Edna relives their summer romance, where more than the weather was hot and steamy, she falls in love all

over again and evokes memories filled with drama, passion, action, and murder.

Tangled Up In Tuesday – Book 4

Organized accountant Zoey Allen likes her life neat and tidy. But it goes from managed to messy when a dead body ends up in her apartment on an ordinary Tuesday night. After uncovering a money-laundering scheme in a routine audit at her company, Zoey finds herself the target in a murderous plot that doesn't quite add up. Good thing she has Mac—a handsome police officer—and the Page Turners book club to help her solve the case.

ABOUT THE AUTHOR

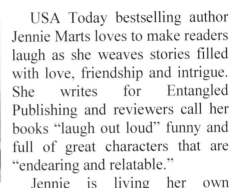 USA Today bestselling author Jennie Marts loves to make readers laugh as she weaves stories filled with love, friendship and intrigue. She writes for Entangled Publishing and reviewers call her books "laugh out loud" funny and full of great characters that are "endearing and relatable."

Jennie is living her own happily-ever-after in the mountains of Colorado with her husband, two sons, two dogs, and a parakeet that loves to tweet to the oldies. She's addicted to Diet Coke, adores Cheetos, and believes you can't have too many books, shoes or friends.

Her books include the contemporary western romance Hearts of Montana series, the romantic comedy/ cozy mysteries of The Page Turners series, the hunky hockey-playing men in the Bannister family in the Bannister Brothers Books, and the small town romantic comedies in the series of Cotton Creek Romances.

Jennie loves to hear from readers. Follow her on Facebook at Jennie Marts Books, Twitter at @JennieMarts, or Goodreads.

Visit her at www.jenniemarts.com and subscribe to her newsletter for the latest happenings and new releases.

** If you enjoyed this book, please consider leaving a review! **
And thanks for reading!

Made in the USA
Coppell, TX
22 March 2020

17369780R00037